George's Marvelous Medicine

KNOPF BOOKS BY ROALD DAHL

Charlie and the Chocolate Factory

Charlie and the Great Glass Elevator

Danny the Champion of the World

The Enormous Crocodile

Fantastic Mr. Fox

George's Marvelous Medicine

James and the Giant Peach

The Mildenhall Treasure

Roald Dahl's Revolting Rhymes

The Wonderful Story of Henry Sugar and Six More